*For my sister, Somyung Kim*

First edition 2021

Library of Congress Catalog Card Number pending
ISBN 978-1-5362-0518-3

21 22 23 24 25 26 APS 10 9 8 7 6 5 4 3 2 1

Printed in Humen, Dongguan, China

This book was typeset in Chaparral.
The illustrations were created with watercolor and digital tools.

Candlewick Press
99 Dover Street
Somerville, Massachusetts 02144

www.candlewick.com

# READY for the SPOTLIGHT!

## Jaime Kim

CANDLEWICK PRESS

I've been taking ballet for a whole month now,
and I think I've got it down!
I'm better than everyone in my class—

everyone except my big sister, Maya.
Maya is always in the spotlight.

Last year she was the Lilac Fairy in *The Sleeping Beauty*, and she even got to wear a crown.

Nobody ever gave me three bouquets of flowers!

"Don't worry, Tessie," says Mom. "When you've been taking ballet as long as Maya, you'll be just as good."

At our next class, I'm ready to go.

"Class, today we'll be learning how to jeté," says the teacher.
"Step forward, raise your right leg, and jump!"

Piece of cake. It looks super easy!
So when she asks who wants to go first,
I raise my hand right away.

See? I'm pretty good.

"Great job, Tessie!" says the teacher.
"But keep practicing. Practice makes perfect."

So I go again. And again!
There are loud cheers and shouts.
Everyone must be applauding me!

No. The applause is for Maya.
She's in the spotlight again.

After class, Mom takes us for ice cream, but I'm still not in a good mood. Today was just not my day. My shoes were slippery. And my tutu felt so heavy. I'm sure that's why I couldn't keep my balance.

At our next class, we have tryouts for the fall recital.
The lead ballerina will be a princess and wear a crown.

I know I'm going to get that part!

Maya is up first. Everyone cheers and claps when she finishes.

When it's my turn, I dance my hardest.

I keep my back straight.

I keep my toes pointed.

After everyone has their turn, we take a break
while the teacher makes the cast list.
It's time to freestyle dance—my favorite!

When the music starts, I swing my hips, waving my hands
and clapping to the music. No rules. No pointed toes.
Who needs lessons when you have rhythm?

Soon everyone is watching me and clapping.
I feel like I've already gotten the lead part.
All I need is a crown and a spotlight!

I keep dancing until the teacher finally returns with the cast list.

"Maya will be the princess. Tessie, Nicole, and Joey will be
the bumblebees. Robin and Mia will be . . ."

It's so unfair!

That night, Maya knocks on my bedroom door.

"Go away!" I shout.

"But I wanted to ask you something, Tessie," says Maya.
"Will you please teach me how to freestyle dance?"

"NO," I say. "You stole my crown."

"You don't need a crown to be a good dancer," she says.
"And anyway, being a bumblebee is one of the most important roles.
When I first started, I was a bumblebee too."

"Really?" I ask. I don't remember that.

"Sure," she says. "Look."

She shows me the bumblebee moves.

"Like this?" I ask.

"Exactly!" she says.

Every night leading up to the recital, Maya and I practice together.

Point, point, wiggle.

Point, point, buzz.

She teaches me how to jump and balance.

And I teach her how to freestyle and groove to the music.

The day of the recital, Maya is still in the spotlight.

But now, so am I.

"You're the best bumblebee I ever saw!" says Maya.

She lets me wear her crown, and suddenly I feel like being a bumblebee is the best thing in the world.

Especially when I have my sister by my side.

And we both get lots of flowers!